This book belongs to

_____

Walt Disney

VOLUME 2

NUMBERS 1-10

WALT DISNEY FUN-TO-LEARN LIBRARY

A BANTAM BOOK
TORONTO • NEW YORK • LONDON • SYDNEY

Numbers 1-10   A Bantam Book/January 1983   All rights reserved. Copyright © 1983 by Walt Disney Productions. This book may not be reproduced, in whole or in part, by mimeograph or any other means.

ISBN 0-553-05502-X

Published simultaneously in the United States and Canada. Bantam Books are published by Bantam Books, Inc. Its trademark, consisting of the words "Bantam Books" and the portrayal of a rooster, is Registered in U.S. Patent and Trademark Office and in other countries. Marca Registrada. Bantam Books, Inc., 666 Fifth Avenue, New York, New York 10103. Printed in the United States of America   0 9 8 7 6 5 4 3 2 1

1
one

"Oh, my goodness! Today I'm giving a surprise birthday party for Mickey, and there's too much work here for just *one* person."

Minnie is right, as you can see. The corn is popping out of its popper. The fudge is bubbling on the stove. The cake is ready to be decorated with a cheery "Happy Birthday, Mickey!" And there is so much more to do!

2
two

Soon there's a *tap! tap!* on Minnie's kitchen door. "Hi, Aunt Minnie," call Morty and Ferdie. "Do you need *two* helpers?"

"You bet I do!" says Minnie. She puts them right to work, filling bowls with popcorn and heaping plates with chocolate-chip cookies.

How many bowls of popcorn do you see?
How many plates of cookies? How many
presents did Morty and Ferdie bring?

3
three

While Morty and Ferdie are helping Minnie in the kitchen, *three* more guests come racing up Minnie's front walk. It is Huey, Dewey, and Louie.

How many presents are Donald's nephews
bringing? How many wheels does Louie's
tricycle have? How many birds do you see?

4
four

Soon Minnie's doorbell rings again. It's a delivery man bringing *four* more presents for Mickey. They're from Donald and Daisy, Grandma Duck, and Uncle Scrooge.

One of the presents the delivery man is bringing has a delicious smell. Grandma must have sent one of her yummy gingerbread men. How many dogs want a piece of Grandma's gingerbread?

Minnie takes the presents inside the house, but the dogs all stay to play in her yard. They bark at the bunny. They chase chipmunks up a tree. They make Huey, Dewey, and Louie laugh.

How many dogs can you count? How many chipmunks
are running up the tree? How many bunnies can you find?
Count the party guests watching from Minnie's window.

One dog jumps onto Huey's fire engine, and it starts to roll. His three friends jump on, too. How many dogs are taking a ride?

But the little fire engine isn't big enough to hold four dogs. One falls off—*kerthump!* How many dogs are still rolling down the path on Huey's red fire engine?

5
five

There are still many things to do for the party. Minnie gives Morty and Ferdie some bright-colored paper. "Here are *five* pieces of paper to make a message for Mickey," she tells them.

They sit down at the party table. Carefully, in their very best printing, they write "Happy" and "Birthday" and "Dear" and "Mickey" and "Mouse." When they put the pieces of paper up on the wall, the message says, "Happy Birthday, Dear Mickey Mouse."

"What a good job you did," says Minnie, coming in from the kitchen. How many party favors is she carrying?

Minnie goes out to pick some shiny red
apples for the party. But what does she find?
"Goats!" cries Minnie. Goats? What are goats
doing in Minnie's yard? How many do you see?

"Farmer Olson must have left his gate open again," Minnie grumbles. She waves her arms at the goats and yells, "Scat!" One of the goats leaps over Minnie's white picket fence. How many goats does Minnie still have to chase away?

6
six

Minnie shuts the gate behind the last goat, but when she turns around, she cries out: "Rabbits! One, two, three, four, five, *six* bunnies munching on my carrots. And crows! Crows climbing all over my scarecrow!"

How many shiny black crows are sitting on the scarecrow? One of them is looking at those ripe, red tomatoes. How many tomatoes can you count on Minnie's vine?

Minnie grabs a rake to chase the bunnies and crows. Four of the bunnies run away, but some try to hide in the garden. How many bunnies are trying to hide from Minnie?

Four of the crows flap away into the sky, too. But there are still some crows looking at Minnie from the scarecrow. How many crows are still in Minnie's garden?

7
seven

At last Minnie is able to pick *seven* shiny red apples. She carries them into the house and puts them on the table.

"Dewey," she calls, "would you please help me set the table?"

How many spoons has Dewey set out? How many bowls is he bringing for the ice cream?

Look! The squirrels who live in Minnie's tree
are peeking in the window. How many can you see?

Minnie has made a pitcher of ice-cold lemonade.
Ferdie has set out the lemonade glasses. Morty is
setting out the party hats. There is a special hat for
Mickey, who will be the guest of honor.

"You boys must be thirsty," says Minnie. "I am, too.
Let's have some lemonade."
　　How many guests can you count? How many party hats do
you see? How many glasses will Minnie fill with lemonade?

8
eight

The party table is almost ready, except for the flowers.

Huey goes out to the garden. "Here are *eight* red roses," he says. "They will make a nice bouquet."

Minnie's kittens watch Huey gather the roses. "Meow?" they say, wondering what Huey is doing.

"A birthday isn't a birthday without flowers," laughs Huey.

How many kittens do you see? How many butterflies?

Morty and Ferdie have gathered a basket of nuts. The squirrels have seen the nuts, too. Squirrels love nuts, so they hop on the porch to eat some. But Morty and Ferdie shoo them away. The squirrels leap off the porch, scattering nuts everywhere.

How many nuts are left in the basket? How many can you find on the porch? How many are there all together?

9
nine

Back in the house, Louie is blowing up balloons. "Boy, am I tired," he says. No wonder Louie is huffing and puffing—he has just blown up *nine* balloons!

Dewey is putting pieces of Minnie's delicious fudge on a plate. How many pieces of fudge do you see?

"Watch out," warns Huey. "The balloons are floating out the window. The wind will blow them away!"

All three boys rush out to bring back the balloons. But Morty and Ferdie are already there.

"We caught the balloons—all but that one," says Morty.

"It's stuck in the tree," adds Ferdie, "and I'm going to get it."

How many balloons did Morty catch? How many birds are watching from the tree?

Now everyone is back in the house. It's time for Mickey to arrive.

When the doorbell rings, Morty, Ferdie, Huey, Dewey, and Louie all scramble for hiding places.

When Minnie opens the door, Mickey can't see any of the guests. But you can. How many are behind the big blue chair? How many are hiding by the party table? How many are using Minnie's yellow sofa to hide?

Boy, is Mickey going to be surprised!

10
ten

"Surprise! Happy birthday!" everyone shouts.

"Wow!" Mickey says. "Is this party all for me?"

"Of course. Happy birthday!" says Minnie.

Minnie is going to cut the birthday cake. "Can anyone
eat two pieces of cake?" she asks.
"I can!" says Huey.
"I can!" says Dewey.
"I can!" says Louie.
So Minnie cuts the cake into *ten* pieces for all her friends.

Look at all the birthday presents! How many are
wrapped in red paper? How many in blue paper?
How many in green? Do you see a very big
present? What could it be?

"There are so many presents to open," Mickey
says. Help him count them. How many are there
altogether?

Mickey's gift from Minnie is a shiny new bicycle. "Uncle Mickey," Morty says, "why don't you try it out?"

"Yes! We can have a parade!" Ferdie adds.

Soon everyone is parading down the street, led by Mickey on his bicycle.

"Thank you, everyone," Mickey says. "This is the best birthday I ever had!"